CR ✓

D0953500

OWEN FOOTE,
MIGHTY SCIENTIST

OWEN FOOTE,
MIGHTY SCIENTIST

by STEPHANIE GREENE

Illustrated by CAT BOWMAN SMITH

SAN DIEGO PUBLIC LIBRARY
CHILDREN'S ROOM

CLARION BOOKS • NEW YORK

3 1336 06923 4509

To John Waszak, a teacher who changes lives
—S. G.

*For my pals Max, Harry, Grant, Adam,
Kai, Devie, Kevin, Allison, Connor, Brendan,
Hannah, Maryn, and Chase*
—C. B. S.

Clarion Books
a Houghton Mifflin Company imprint
215 Park Avenue South, New York, NY 10003
Text copyright © 2004 by Stephanie Greene
Illustrations copyright © 2004 by Cat Bowman Smith

The text was set in 13.5-point Palatino.
The illustrations were executed in pen and ink.

All rights reserved.

For information about permission to reproduce selections from this book,
write to Permissions, Houghton Mifflin Company,
215 Park Avenue South, New York, NY 10003.

www.houghtonmifflinbooks.com

Printed in the U.S.A.

Library of Congress Cataloging-in-Publication Data
Greene, Stephanie.
Owen Foote, mighty scientist / by Stephanie Greene ; illustrated by
Catherine Bowman Smith.
p. cm.
Summary: Third-grade best friends Owen and Joseph struggle to come up
with a great science fair project that they will both enjoy doing; then something
goes wrong and they have to change their plans two days before the fair.
ISBN 0-618-43016-4
[1. Science projects—Fiction. 2. Tadpoles—Fiction. 3. Lizards as pets—Fiction.
4. Best friends—Fiction. 5. Friendship—Fiction. 6. Schools—Fiction.]
I. Smith, Cat Bowman, ill. II. Title.
PZ7.G8434Out 2004
[Fic]—dc22   2003027072

ISBN-13: 978-0-618-43016-1   ISBN-10: 0-618-43016-4

QUM 10 9 8 7 6 5 4 3 2 1

CONTENTS

1

"Those Are the Ones I Want"

"Those," said Owen. He pointed to the small gray lizards in the aquarium labeled UROMASTYX.

"Those are the ones I want," he said.

"I don't even know how to say it," said Joseph.

"It's *euro*, like in *Europe*," Owen told him. "Euro-mass-ticks."

Owen was staring at the pile of squirming lizards that were trying to claw their way to the top of the heap over one another's backs. Their beaklike mouths looked razor-sharp. Their wide, flat tails were covered with plates like armor.

Every one of their toes had a long, pointy nail at the end of it.

They were the most incredible things Owen had ever seen.

"They look like prehistoric monsters," Joseph said uneasily.

"I know. Aren't they great?"

As they watched, one of the largest lizards finally fought its way to the top of the writhing pile. It teetered for a second with its leg extended toward the lip of the aquarium. Then it toppled backwards and slid to the bottom.

It got to its feet and began fighting its way to the top again.

"I'd have nightmares if I kept one of those in my room," said Joseph.

Owen reached out to pet one of the smaller lizards sitting in one corner of the aquarium. It swiveled its head around when it saw his finger coming and stared up at it expectantly.

"See how intelligent it is?" he said. "I think it already knows me."

"*I* think it's about to bite you," said Joseph.

"No, these guys are really friendly. I've read about them." Owen touched the lizard's back lightly with his finger. The lizard made a dash for the other side of the aquarium.

"Come on, Owen." Joseph tugged at Owen's sleeve. "Your mom said half an hour, remember?"

Owen looked up at the bleachers. He had forgotten all about his mom. She had followed him and Joseph around the Reptile and Amphibian Show for a while. Then she said she was going to read while she waited for them.

Owen couldn't understand how anyone could read when they could be petting a lizard. But as much as he had encouraged her, his mom didn't seem to want to touch anything.

"I don't know, Owen," she had said when he dragged her over to look at a huge white frog with pink eyes and a stomach that oozed out around it like a plate. "Some of these things make me a little queasy."

"I know what you mean," said Joseph.

"Want to wait with me, Joseph?" Owen's mom said with a smile.

"Are you kidding?" Owen threw his arm around Joseph's shoulders. "Joseph's no wimp. He loves this stuff as much as I do. Except the snakes—right, Joseph?"

"Right."

Owen and Joseph had kept going. They stopped at dozens of tables. Looked at all kinds of animals. There were tarantulas with hairy legs. Colorful poison dart frogs. Millipedes that looked like huge cockroaches. A swamp turtle shaped like a leaf.

Owen had seen lots of them before. It was his third show. But it was Joseph's first time. Owen had promised him they would avoid the snakes. He hadn't counted on the four-hundred-pound boa constrictor curled up on the floor inside a playpen by the front door.

He thought Joseph was going to faint when he saw it.

Owen pulled him away from it as quickly as he could, but Joseph's face hadn't lost its mildly terrified expression ever since. Owen usually would have noticed. Today he was too busy peering.

To Owen, every table was more interesting than the one before. The lizards interested him the most.

He couldn't get enough of them.

He stopped at every lizard table. He asked questions and read pamphlets. They had stopped at the uromastyx table earlier. Now they were back. This time, Owen wasn't budging.

Joseph looked at his watch for the fourth time. "Really, Owen. It's late."

"Now I know what they remind me of," Owen said. "Miniature Triceratops without the horns."

When he was in kindergarten, Owen had wanted to study dinosaurs when he grew up. He loved how huge dinosaurs were. How ferocious. But after a while he realized they were all dead.

Owen didn't want to study animals that were dead. He wanted to study animals that were alive. Animals that ate and burrowed and swam and grew.

Weird animals that looked exotic.

Dangerous, even.

The kind of animal that would make your sister scream if it got loose in her room.

A uromastyx.

"What if those guys are man-eaters?" Joseph said. He sounded nervous. "My mom might not let me spend the night at your house again."

"I'm almost positive they're vegetarians," said Owen. He looked at the man in the muscle shirt behind the table. He had a long blond pony tail and an eyebrow ring. The snake tattoo that started at his shoulder wound down around his arm to his wrist.

Owen had noticed that a lot of the people at the Reptile and Amphibian Show had tattoos. And earrings in places other than their ears. And T-shirts with glow-in-the-dark reptile designs.

"Excuse me," Owen said.

The man put down the brochures he was folding and came over to them. "What can I do for you boys?" he said.

"How big will the uromastyx get?" said Owen. It made him feel mature, saying a word like *uromastyx*. He didn't sound like a little kid who was excited about lizards.

He sounded like someone who knew something.

"About a foot long." The man held his hands apart. "Maybe five or six pounds."

"A whole *foot?*" Joseph said.

"They're vegetarians, right?" said Owen.

"Right. They eat mostly green stuff. The darker, the better. Kale, spinach, romaine . . . anything but iceberg," said the man. "It's nothing but water."

"That's what my mother always says," said Owen. "My dad loves iceberg, but she won't let him eat it."

His fist had closed around the wad of bills in his pocket while they talked. All he had was fifteen dollars. So far the only things he'd seen that he could afford were turtles and newts.

Joseph had a turtle. Owen would never say it, but he thought turtles were kind of boring. Nice, but boring. And Owen had gotten two newts last summer. When he first got them, they were really exciting. Now they weren't enough. Compared with lizards, newts were like a bicycle with training wheels.

Baby stuff.

He looked at the man hopefully. "How much do they cost?"

"Twenty dollars."

Owen was crushed.

"Too bad," said Joseph. He sounded relieved. "At least you won't get salmonella," he added helpfully.

Owen was too busy thinking to listen. If his mom lent him five dollars, he could do it. He'd promise to clean his room without having to be told. And take out the garbage. And clean his bathroom. . . .

Wait a minute—no need to go crazy here.

"Thanks," he said abruptly. "Come on, Joseph."

Owen slipped between the couple standing behind them and took off. By the time Joseph caught up with him, he was coming back down the bleachers with his mom in tow.

"Wait till you see them," he was saying. "You'll fall in love with them."

"I wouldn't bet on it, Owen," she said. "How much do they cost?"

"The man said they're really intelligent. And they don't bite, like some lizards." Owen kept talking as fast as he could. He knew his mom. If he told her how much they cost, she'd make up her mind right here and now. But if she saw the uromastyx first, she might just fall in love with them.

Then they could talk money.

It worked. Maybe his mom wasn't madly in *love,* but she liked them. He could tell.

"They *are* kind of interesting," she said, looking into the aquarium. "They're like something out of a science fiction movie."

"Feeding them is no problem," Owen said quickly. "All they eat is lettuce. But not iceberg. You were right about that one, Mom. Iceberg's nothing but water."

"Flattery will get you nowhere," his mom said dryly. But she was smiling. Owen felt a glimmer of hope.

"How big do they get?" she asked.

"It'll fit in my twenty-gallon aquarium, easy," said Owen. "You're lucky I don't want an iguana. They get to be five feet long. People have to build special shelves for them all over the house so they can wander around."

"Spare me that," said Mrs. Foote. Then her expression changed. From the look in her eyes Owen could tell the Big Question was coming.

"How much?" she asked again.

"Twenty dollars." Owen held up his wad of money. "All I need to borrow is five dollars."

"Oh, Owen." His mom wasn't smiling anymore. "That seems like a lot of money—"

"Please, Mom? I might want to be a herpetologist when I grow up. I need to start studying these things."

His mom's mouth had settled into the thin line that meant no. "I thought you wanted to be a paleontologist," she said.

"Not anymore," said Owen. "I love lizards. You know I do. I've loved them since I got Socrates and Plato last year. I've read a million books about them."

"Yes, but twenty dollars?"

"Please?" Owen pleaded. "I'll pay you back."

His mom looked at him for a long minute. Finally, she sighed.

"What if you decide you want to be a marine biologist?" she said. "Will we have to buy you a whale?"

It took Owen only a second to pick the lizard he wanted. The small one in the corner. It had finally

stopped running away from him. Now when Owen reached out to pet it, it cocked its head to one side and stared back with one bright eye.

The man put it in a box with a clear lid and gave Owen a pamphlet on uromastyx.

Owen and Joseph followed Mrs. Foote out to the car.

"What are you going to name him?" Joseph asked.

"I was thinking about Chuck," said Owen.

"Chuck?" Mrs. Foote laughed. "Isn't that kind of a strange choice after Plato and Socrates?"

"Chuck's not as thoughtful as those two," Owen said. "I can tell. If he was a kid, he'd like football."

"Good heavens," said his mom. "How can you tell?"

"I know these things," Owen said.

"How do you know it's a boy?" said Joseph.

"It just feels like one."

Joseph had a point, though. Owen had forgotten to ask the man what Chuck was. But he didn't want to lift up a lizard he hardly knew and peer at its naked belly. It felt kind of rude.

"I'll check in my book to make sure," he said. "If it's a girl, I'll call her Carlotta."

"If . . . ," said Mrs. Foote as she opened the car door, ". . . you promise to feed Chuck and give him fresh water and clean his cage once a week—"

"Defecatoria," said Owen. He slid onto the back seat with the box balanced carefully in his lap. "Uromastyx are very neat. They only poop in one area of their cage. It's called the defecatoria."

"Defecatoria, then," said Mrs. Foote. She fixed him with a beady eye in the rearview mirror. "*If* you do all of that without being reminded, Owen, you can consider the five dollars a gift."

"Thanks, Mom," he said. "You can be Chuck's grandmother. And you can be his godfather, Joseph. I'll let you hold him when we get home."

"I don't mind waiting," Joseph said quickly. "You should probably bond with him first."

"Good idea," said Owen. "It would be terrible if he thought you were his father instead of me."

"You can say that again," said Joseph.

2

Lab Coats, Here We Come!

"Boys and girls?" Mrs. McBride grabbed a stack of paper from her desk and waved it in the air above her head. "Before you leave, I'm going to hand out the information about the science fair."

Owen flashed Joseph a quick look across the aisle and made the thumbs-up sign. He had been waiting for this all year.

"Make sure you show this to your parents," their teacher said. "The science fair is in three weeks. Mr. Wozniak would like to have as many of you as possible participate." She handed everyone a paper as she moved slowly down the aisle toward Owen. "There will be sessions in the library after school for those of you who need help. Volunteers will be there to help you get started.

"The important thing to remember," she went on in a loud voice as she handed Owen his copy, "is that you need to come up with a project you can do on your own or as a team. It's fine if your parents want to give you a bit of help. But *you* need to be the one who does the work."

"Try telling that to Anthony," Owen muttered.

Last year Anthony did a project on astronomy. His father took the photographs with his expensive telescope. He typed the descriptions below them, too. It looked as if all Anthony had done was sign his name.

Thinking about the second prize Anthony won still made Owen mad. If judges couldn't tell the difference between a project a kid did by himself and one his parents did for him, they should let kids be the judges.

Kids could tell every time.

He quickly scanned the notice Mrs. McBride had handed him. It had dates and rules and information about prizes. Words like *hypothesis* and *scientific method* were written in bold type.

Owen could hardly wait to get home and read it. He loved the science fair. Chesterfield School had held it for the first time when he was in the first grade. Owen could still remember how amazing the projects had seemed to him.

Last year he and Joseph did a project on evaporation. It embarrassed Owen every time he thought about how babyish it had been. Neither of them had cared that it didn't win anything.

They were only in the second grade. They still thought working for nothing was fun.

This year was different.

This year Owen *had* to win a prize. If he didn't, Mr. Wozniak would never know who Owen was. How much Owen loved science.

He wouldn't pick Owen to be in his fourth-grade class.

Owen knew that if he didn't get into Mr. Wozniak's class, he would die.

Lots of kids who liked science wanted to be in that class. Owen didn't just *want* to be there. He felt as if he *belonged* there.

When it came to science, there wasn't another teacher in Chesterfield School like Mr. Wozniak. Or another classroom like his. Every time Owen walked past it, he felt as though he was walking past a magic place.

A sign over the door said LAND OF WOZ. There was a rainbow above it. And a picture of a wizard with a peaked hat and a wand.

Mr. Wozniak's students were called *Wizards*. The ones who followed the class rules and worked hard were awarded a special Wizard pass. It allowed them to stay inside at recess and play chess if they wanted. Even walk to the media center by themselves.

The classroom walls were lined with aquariums. A tiger salamander named Elliot lived in one. Next to him was Big Mac, a yellow-bellied slider. Then Boinky, a huge box turtle. There were lizards and newts and snakes.

And in one, a lone frog named Hip.

"It was Hip and Hop," one of the Wizards told Owen's class last year when they were touring Critter Island. "But Hop ran away."

To Owen, Critter Island was the most special part of it all. Mr. Wozniak's class built it every year. First, they pushed all the tables together and covered them with plywood. Then they took shredded newspaper and flour and water and made papier-mâché. They built mountains and streams and lakes.

They painted trees and grass and water.

Then all the Wizards chose an animal they liked and studied it until they were experts. When the younger classes came in for a tour during the last week of school, the Wizards stood around in white lab coats and talked about their animals.

Owen could still remember how it felt to file into that room. How cool the Wizards looked in their white lab coats. To him, they looked like real scientists. He had been dreaming about wearing one of those coats ever since. He didn't think he could bear it if he got into any other fourth-grade class.

Like Mrs. Grady's class. Or Ms. Holt's.

Mrs. Grady loved English. The kids read a lot of books and wrote one of their own. They even had a real author come for a visit. Ms. Holt's class put on a play every year. They sang and danced in front of the whole school.

After Joseph was in a play at camp, he talked

about maybe being in Ms. Holt's class. But Owen knew he could talk him out of it. Especially once they won a prize at the science fair and Mr. Wozniak picked them for his class.

Owen folded his paper and put it in his pack. No way was he going to write a book. Or sing and dance in front of the whole school. He was going to talk about lizards in a white lab coat. Little kids in the lower grades were going to stare at him when he walked by.

When the bell rang, he slung his pack over his shoulder and got into line behind Joseph. They started snaking their way toward the door.

"We'd better get to work right away," Owen said.

"Maybe we should go to the library and get a few books," said Joseph.

"We don't need books. I've got tons of ideas."

"I already know what I'm going to do," said Anthony. He squeezed into line in front of Joseph. "My father's going to help me analyze blood samples. We're going to take photographs of cells and everything."

"You don't know anything about blood samples," Owen said. "That's your father's job."

"So?"

"You heard Mrs. McBride," Joseph said. "We're supposed to do something by ourselves."

"I will," said Anthony. "My dad will watch."

"Yeah, right," Owen said. "Come on, Joseph. We don't need our parents to do *our* project."

He shouldered his way past Anthony and started down the hall.

"What are you guys doing?" Anthony called.

"We haven't decided yet," shouted Owen.

It wasn't until he turned into his driveway that it came to him. He and Joseph didn't have to waste time thinking of an idea. Owen already had one. The greatest science project in the whole world was sitting in his bedroom.

Chuck.

Owen could see it all now. A blue ribbon on his project. Mr. Wozniak leading Owen under the rainbow into his room.

Chuck sitting calmly on the shoulder of Owen's white lab coat while kindergarteners gazed at them with open mouths.

White lab coats, here we come! Owen thought excitedly.

He could hardly wait to tell Joseph.

3

Lizard Talk

"Hi, Mom."

Owen flung his pack onto a chair and put his lunch box beside the sink. "We got an announcement about the science fair. It's in three weeks. Joseph's coming over so him and me can decide what project to do."

"He and I," his mother corrected.

"Right." Owen opened the refrigerator and pulled out the vegetable drawer. "Actually, I already thought of a great idea. Want to hear it?"

"Don't you think you should talk it over with Joseph first?" said Mrs. Foote. "You *are* a team."

"Good idea." Owen grabbed a handful of lettuce, shut the drawer with his foot, and let the door close.

"How many times have I asked you not to use your feet?" said his mom.

"About a million." Lydia brushed past Owen and stuck her pencil in the electric sharpener next to the phone. "Owen never listens to what you say," she yelled over the noise.

"I just pushed it," Owen said.

Lydia blew on the sharpened point and glared at the lettuce in Owen's hand. "What are you trying to do, starve that horrible thing to death?"

"If you really want to know, one of the biggest reasons reptiles die is because of overfeeding," Owen said.

"Even so, Lydia may have a point," said Mrs. Foote. "Chuck's getting kind of big. Don't you think you should give him a little more than that?"

"Trust me, Mom. I know what I'm doing," Owen said. "He doesn't get any exercise. I don't want him to get fat."

"Can a lizard get fat on lettuce?" said his mom.

"Owen thinks that just because *he* eats like a bird, everybody else should, too," Lydia said. "That's why he's such a shrimp."

"Lydia, that was uncalled for," said Mrs. Foote.

"At least I'm not *fat*, like some people," said Owen.

"At least I don't look like a skeleton."

"Fatty."

"Bony."

"Stop. Both of you," said Mrs. Foote. "Lydia, didn't you tell me you had homework to do?"

"That's right, take Owen's side," Lydia said. "You always do."

"What's bugging her?" said Owen as Lydia's bedroom door slammed.

"She's not in a very good mood right now," said his mom.

"She's never in a very good mood," said Owen. "What's wrong with her this time?"

His mom sighed. "Remember how she and Kate auditioned for the spring concert last week?"

"Yeah."

"Lydia found out today that Kate got in and she didn't."

"So? Kate can sing and she can't," said Owen. "What's the big deal?"

"Kate's her best friend," said Mrs. Foote. "Try to

imagine how you'd feel if it happened to you and Joseph."

"Me and Joseph?" Owen scoffed. "Boys don't get into dumb things like that."

"Boys have feelings, too, you know," said his mom.

"Not about dumb stuff like that, they don't." Owen headed for the stairs. "Send Joseph up when he comes, okay?"

Lydia had her music on full blast. Owen considered pounding on her door as he went past but didn't. The last thing he needed was for her to come into his room to retaliate.

He wanted to be alone to think.

He shut his door and went over to the aquarium. Chuck was lying on his heat rock. When Owen lifted up the lid, Chuck darted across the sand and hid under the bridge Owen had made out of rocks.

"Hi, Chuck," Owen said. "Dinnertime."

He dropped the lettuce onto the sand. Chuck darted out, latched onto a piece, and dragged it back to his hiding place. He chomped away at it with short, jerky bites, like he was mad.

Owen sat back and watched him. He had been trying to bond with Chuck for a few weeks now. He wasn't sure Chuck liked him yet.

Bonding with the newts had been easy. Chuck was different. Nothing Owen did calmed him down. Owen tried talking in a soothing voice. Stroking Chuck's back. Fixing rocks for him to climb on. Picking him up.

The picking him up part was the worst. All the books said that the more you handled a lizard, the more relaxed it became. That's the way it had been with Socrates and Plato.

Not with Chuck.

Every time Owen picked Chuck up, he thrashed his legs and whipped his tail back and forth. Owen put him back down, fast. He *knew* Chuck's tail couldn't hurt him, but it looked pretty threatening.

The bigger Chuck got, the more threatening it looked.

Taking care of him was harder than Owen had expected. He'd never admit it, but Chuck made him just a *tiny* bit nervous. He wasn't going to give up, though. Especially now, when there was so much riding on it.

Chuck finished the lettuce and crawled back onto his heat rock.

"Good boy, that's a good boy," Owen said softly. He reached in and ran his finger gently along Chuck's back. One time. Then another. And another.

Chuck's eyes slid slowly shut. His body seemed to relax. Owen kept stroking his back. He talked in a low voice. Maybe Chuck was at least beginning to recognize his voice, he thought.

Maybe using a certain tone of voice was the secret.

Owen had looked through his books to see if there was a certain way of talking that calmed lizards down.

"Lizard talk" or something.

Owen sat back on his heels in amazement. That was it!

Lizard talk. *That* could be their project. Maybe he and Joseph could prove you could train a lizard to recognize different voices. Maybe Chuck could learn to eat when Owen talked to him. And lie down when Joseph talked to him.

Maybe they could even get him to do tricks.

The more Owen thought about it, the more excited he got. He jumped up to get a pencil and some paper just as his door opened.

It was Joseph.

"My mother said she can drive us to the library," he said. He sat down on the edge of Owen's bed. "Wow. Chuck's getting big."

"He grew two inches already," Owen said. "Seven more and he'll be a foot."

He was so excited he could hardly sit still.

"I got the greatest idea, Joseph," he said as he lifted the lid. "It's so cool. Wait till you hear it."

"Wait a minute, Owen," said Joseph. He slid back on the bed as Owen picked a squirming Chuck out of his aquarium. His eyes were glued to Chuck's thrashing legs. "If your idea is about Chuck, maybe I should work on something by myself."

"Are you joking? We always work together," Owen said. "See? There's nothing to it." He put Chuck in the palm of his hand and stroked his back firmly. Calm down, Chuck, he pleaded silently. Please. For once, calm down.

"You just have to keep a firm grip on him," he said. "If you pet his back long enough, he stops kicking."

"No, thanks." Joseph crossed his arms over his chest. "I don't want to get salmonella."

"See? He's calming down already," said Owen. He felt a rush of gratitude for the way Chuck had suddenly relaxed. He was lying quietly in Owen's hand. The sides of his stomach were billowing gently in and out, in and out.

He was staring straight ahead. It looked as if he was waiting for something.

Owen felt giddy with relief. "I told you, there's nothing to it."

Then what Chuck was waiting for arrived.

His sides suddenly ballooned out, his body gave a convulsive shake, and he pooped. A warm, slippery, greenish-black poop with white stuff at one end slid out onto Owen's hand.

Owen stared at it in disbelief.

This was not the dry, harmless poop he scooped out of Plato's and Socrates' cage. This was disgusting. And it was sitting on his hand.

"Gross!" Joseph shouted. He jumped up off the bed and ran to the other side of the room. "That stuff is riddled with germs!"

Owen dumped Chuck back into his aquarium and shook his hand. The poop slid onto the rug at his feet. He grabbed a Kleenex and scrubbed his hand as hard as he could.

The trick was not to think about it. He wanted to shout and yell and dunk his hand in sulfuric acid. But he knew he had to stay calm.

He couldn't let Joseph knew how grossed out he was.

Joseph was plastered up against the wall as if he was expecting the poop to attack him. Owen looked at him and shrugged. "It's no big deal," he lied.

"Oh, yes, it is," said Joseph. His voice was trembling. "Don't you ever ask me to touch that lizard again. I mean it. That's the most disgusting thing I've ever seen."

"Okay, okay. Calm down."

Owen grabbed another Kleenex and a small plastic bag and crouched down. Chuck's little surprise didn't look any better the second time

around. Owen took a deep breath and grabbed it.

When he felt its squishy softness under his fingers, he almost shrieked. Instead, he stuffed the poop into the bag and held it away from his body with the tips of his fingers.

"I'll be right back," he said.

He bolted past Joseph and down the hall to the bathroom. He slammed the door and threw the bag into the trash. Then he put his hand under the faucet and turned the hot water on, full blast.

He couldn't believe how grossed out he was. He'd thought he could take anything that had to do with lizards. But a wet poop?

Owen didn't think he could bear it if Chuck did that to him again.

He stared at himself in the mirror above the sink. Maybe Joseph wasn't the only one who never wanted to pick Chuck up. Owen wasn't sure he wanted to, either. But he couldn't worry about it now. He had more pressing problems.

Like the science fair. If he and Joseph were still going to win, they had to come up with another idea.

And fast.

4

"Eureka!"

"What are you doing?" said Joseph.

Owen looked up from the floor of the garage. He was lying on his side with his knees pulled up to his chest. A length of thin wire was wound around his left wrist and his left ankle. The end of the wire was attached to a nine-volt battery.

There was a pile of nails on the floor next to his head.

"I'm trying to turn myself into a human battery," he said, "but it's not working."

He lowered his head until the tip of his nose touched the top of the pile. Then he lifted it up slowly, hoping to drag a few of the nails along with him.

The end of his nose remained empty.

"Darn!" Owen sat up and started to unwind the wire from around his leg. "I thought maybe it would work. I bet they've never seen a human battery at the science fair before."

"It sounds more like something you'd see at a carnival," Joseph said. "Like the one last summer where we saw the Smallest Horse in the World."

"You mean the normal-sized pony they put in a pit so we were taller than it."

"It looked pretty small." Joseph knelt down to help Owen put the nails back into their box. "Maybe the nails are too heavy," he said.

"I tried paper clips," said Owen. "That didn't work, either."

"You probably need a lot more power than a nine-volt battery."

"Yeah, but then I'd electrocute myself." Owen got up off the floor and bunched the wire into a tight ball.

"Maybe we should forget the human part," Joseph said. "We could use other materials like water and wood and—"

"That's boring," Owen said impatiently. "Everyone does stuff like that. There'll probably be about ten volcanoes and a hundred solar systems."

He tossed the tangle of wire back on the shelf in disgust.

He and Joseph had been trying for days to think of a good idea. All they'd come up with were boring projects anyone could do. Joseph thought some of them were fine.

Owen didn't.

Their project needed to *prove* something, he thought restlessly. He looked around the garage. It needed to involve something alive. Something that would make it special. More than just looking up facts and writing them down. Or drawing pictures and pasting them onto a presentation board.

His eyes swept over the tools and gardening stuff and bicycles littering the garage. They stopped on the pile of fishing gear next to his dad's workbench.

Wait a minute.

Owen gazed at the small white container with holes in the side. His bait bucket. It was sitting next to the gray bucket he and his dad used for fishing.

It was the same bucket Owen used every spring when he went down to the swamp.

"That's it!" he shouted, rushing toward it. "I can't believe I didn't think of it before!"

"Think of what?" said Joseph.

"The swamp. I bet there are millions of them." Owen grabbed the gray bucket off the pile and held it out to Joseph.

"Millions of what?" said Joseph.

"Frog eggs," Owen said. He grabbed a white net off a hook. "The swamp at the back of Mrs. Gold's property is full of them this time of year, remember? Come on."

He ran out of the garage and around the side of the house. They had a little less than two weeks, he thought as he led the way across the lawn. The peepers had been going crazy for the past week. Owen heard them every night when he got into bed.

If the eggs were far enough along, they'd hatch into tadpoles in a few days.

Then what?

"Remember how many we hatched last year?" he said over his shoulder as they cut into the woods. "We must have had a million of them. It's perfect."

"We can draw a diagram of their growth cycle," said Joseph, "and explain the stages and everything."

"That's baby stuff," Owen said as they went past his tree fort at a full trot. "You read what Mr. Wozniak wrote. A really good experiment has to have a hypothesis. You have to set up a question and then find the answer."

"He didn't say we *had* to," panted Joseph. The bucket was banging against his leg as he hurried to keep up. "He said we *could*. Most kids won't have one."

"That's why we have to." Owen veered off the path to the right and began pushing his way through a tangle of bushes. Prickers tore at his shirt. Honeysuckle vine wound itself around his ankles. He let a branch snap back and heard Joseph say, "Ouch."

"Sorry," Owen said. He didn't stop or turn around.

Usually, he went more slowly. He knew Joseph had a hard time with the vines. And he always held the branch so it wouldn't snap back and hit the person behind him. But Owen didn't have time for any of that now. He had to get to the swamp and see if they had a science project.

Let them be there, he pleaded silently as he broke through into the clearing. Please let them be there. He narrowed his eyes and scanned the swamp in front of him.

It was dotted with rotting tree trunks and fallen trees. The beaver lodge he and Joseph had walked out to when the swamp was frozen was bigger than ever. Chewed trees that looked like pencils lined the bank.

In the early spring when the peepers were mating, the sound was deafening. Today it was quiet. Owen was searching the surface of the stagnant water when Joseph came crashing out onto the bank behind him. He doubled over with his hands on his knees to catch his breath.

"Do you see any?" he said breathlessly.

Owen shook his head. Maybe they were too late. Maybe the snakes and turtles had eaten them all. He turned toward the *plop!* a frog made as it leapt off the bank into the water to his left.

That's when he saw it. A mass of cloudy jelly dotted with tiny black specks. It was wedged between a rock and a stick beneath the surface of the water.

"Eureka!" Owen shouted.

He twirled around and punched Joseph on the shoulder. This must have been what Lewis and Clark felt like when they saw the ocean, he thought excitedly. Or maybe Ben Franklin when he discovered electricity.

"You get the water," he told Joseph. "I'll snag it with the net."

"Maybe we should go home and get our boots first," said Joseph.

"Don't be such a wimp," said Owen. He stuck his net out and started prodding the mass of eggs. Joseph crouched down on the bank and held the bucket in the water near the eggs.

The eggs were slippery. They kept bobbing away from Owen's net in the shallow water. Every time he started to lift them out slowly, they slipped back over the edge of the net. They were floating farther and farther away from the bank.

"What are you doing, Joseph?" Owen said. "Bring the bucket closer."

He grabbed a root sticking out of the bank and leaned out as far as he could. Cold water seeped into his shoes and surrounded his toes. The dense smell of mud was heavy in the air.

"I can't go any farther," Joseph said next to him. "My sneakers will get wet."

The eggs slipped back into the water again. "Darn!" Owen sat back and felt a cold shock as the water met the seat of his pants. "So?" he said impatiently. "Let them get wet. If we don't get these things, we have no experiment."

"It's just that they're kind of new," said Joseph. Owen turned to look at him. Joseph had a streak of mud on his forehead where he had scratched. A small twig was sticking up out of his hair like a horn.

Joseph hated being dirty. Owen knew he was miserable. But right now he really didn't care.

"Just hold the bucket closer," he said, grabbing the root again. "I'll push the eggs into it."

Joseph hesitated. Then he stepped into the water and tipped the bucket closer to the eggs.

This time it worked. Owen pushed the eggs safely over the rim and Joseph tilted it upright.

Together they lifted the bucket onto the bank and sat down on either side of it. Owen was wet and dirty, but happy. Even Joseph looked excited.

"How many do you think we got?" he said. "It looks like a lot."

They peered at the inert blob floating in the bucket. It looked like a huge, dirty jellyfish with black chicken pox.

"There isn't much going on now, but there will be soon," said Owen. Any day now, the specks would start twitching. Tiny tadpoles would work their way free of the jelly like dancing commas.

Owen had seen it happen every year. It always amazed him.

He stuck his finger into the water and frowned. "It's freezing. We'd better get this into my room to speed things up. I can put it near the radiator."

They started back through the woods, carrying the bucket between them. Owen was short and Joseph was tall. No matter how carefully they walked, dirty water sloshed up over the sides of the bucket with every step.

By the time they reached the path they were sopping wet from the knees down.

"Maybe that could be our experiment," Owen said as they staggered along. "We could put some of the eggs in hot water to see if they hatch faster. And maybe some in the freezer."

"That would kill them," said Joseph. "I don't think we should hurt them just for a science experiment."

Owen didn't respond. He had suddenly remembered two photographs he saw in his nature magazine a few months ago. One was of a two-headed snake.

The other one was of a frog with three legs.

He hadn't shown them to Joseph. Joseph didn't even like photographs of normal snakes. Owen knew a picture of a snake with two heads, shaped like a "Y" at the top, would freak him out.

But Owen had been fascinated. The article with the photographs talked about the effects of fertilizers and pesticides on nature. It said chemicals were seeping into underground waterways. That animals in streams and ponds were growing up deformed.

Farmers and large companies weren't the only ones doing it, the article said. Gardeners all over the United States were guilty.

Gardeners like his dad, Owen suddenly realized. In his mind's eye he could see the fertilizer his dad sprinkled on their lawn. The bag was leaning against the garage wall behind the lawnmower.

Owen was so excited, he tripped over a root. A sweep of dirty water slopped up over the sides of the bucket like a tidal wave.

"Hey, watch it!" Joseph yelled.

They put the bucket down and looked at their feet.

"My mom's going to kill me," said Joseph.

Joseph's new sneakers were more brown than white. His shoelaces were caked with mud. Owen felt a pang of guilt.

"Mine are wet, too," he said.

"Yeah, but yours are old. Besides, your mom doesn't care." Joseph picked up the bucket. "It'll be easier if I carry this by myself."

Owen held the branches carefully as he led the way through the woods. It probably wasn't the best time to tell Joseph about his idea, he realized. He would work it out by himself first. Then he'd tell him.

It *definitely* wasn't the right time to bring up the photographs.

Owen wasn't sure whether Joseph would be more freaked out by a lizard that pooped in your hand or by a three-legged frog.

He bet it would be a close race.

5

All Handfuls Aren't the Same

Owen dumped his wet sneakers in the mudroom and burst into the kitchen. It was empty. He ran into the family room. His mom was standing in front of the picture window.

"Guess what?" he said. "We finally got an idea for our science project."

"Hi, Owen. I'm glad you're home." Mrs. Foote turned around. Owen realized she was standing in front of Chuck's aquarium. Owen had moved it into the family room the day before. He said Chuck needed more light.

"I think Chuck might be sick," his mom said.

Something thumped in the bottom of Owen's stomach. "He's okay," he said.

"I don't think he is." His mom turned back to

Chuck. "I looked at him when I got home from work. He doesn't look good."

Owen didn't move. "He'll be okay."

"Owen?" said his mom. She sounded puzzled. As if she expected him to act more concerned. Rush to Chuck's side or something, instead of just stand there.

"Would you come over here, please, and tell me if you think there's something wrong?" she said.

Owen didn't have to look to see if something was wrong. He knew there was. Something had been wrong for about a week. That was why he had brought Chuck downstairs.

Chuck had been acting listless. He had practically stopped eating.

His stomach, though, kept getting fatter and fatter. It had started to look like a balloon. Owen was terrified he was going to be woken up one night by the sound of Chuck exploding. Even though he knew Chuck was sick, he hadn't picked him up to check.

Owen hadn't picked Chuck up since that day with Joseph.

He walked slowly across the room and stood

next to his mom. It was just as he had feared. The balloon was ready to explode.

"Has he been eating normally?" his mom said, crouching down to get a better look.

"Kind of." Owen shrugged uneasily. "Actually, not really."

"What does 'not really' mean?" she said impatiently.

"He hasn't eaten anything."

"That's what I thought." His mom stood up. "I think we'd better take him to that reptile hospital you got the name of. When an animal stops eating, it means there's something wrong."

"I can't go now," Owen said. "Joseph and I got tadpoles. I have to—"

His mom cut him off.

"Correct me if I'm wrong, Owen," she said, "but a few weeks ago you thought getting Chuck was the most important thing in the world."

"It was."

"Then before you start taking on more animals, you need to take care of the ones you already have," she said. "What's going on here?"

Owen looked at his feet. He didn't know how to

explain it. He didn't really understand it himself. Ever since Chuck's "accident," things had changed.

Owen didn't trust Chuck anymore. He didn't want to train him. Or get to know him. Or hold him.

He especially didn't want to hold him. And that made him feel like a wimp.

"You don't want him to die, do you?" said his mom.

"Want who to die?" said Lydia. She dumped her armload of books onto a chair and came over to where they were standing. "Wow. Owen was right. A lizard *can* get fat on lettuce."

"He's not fat, he's sick," said Mrs. Foote. "Owen and I are taking him to the vet. If we're not back by five, please put the meatloaf in the oven at three-fifty."

She picked up her car keys from the coffee table. "Come on, Owen. Let's go."

*   *   *

"He was what?" Lydia said blankly.

"Bound." Mrs. Foote took off her coat and draped it over the back of the couch. Owen opened the small cardboard box with Chuck inside and dumped him into the aquarium. Chuck made an angry dash for his cave.

"What's that supposed to mean?" said Lydia. She looked from her mom to Owen and back to her mom again.

"Oh, my gosh." She put her hands over her mouth. "That is *so* gross. You mean constipated, don't you?"

"Lydia, please," sighed Mrs. Foote. "I've had about all I can take for one day."

"It does! It means constipated! That is *so* disgusting!" Lydia started hopping up and down and flapping her hands in front of her face as if she was trying to fly. "Gross! I can't stand it! I think I'm going to throw up! That is so gross!"

Suddenly, she stopped. She looked back and forth between her mother and Owen again. "You had to give him a laxative, didn't you?"

This time she didn't wait for the answer.

"That is so *gross*!" she shrieked at the top of her lungs. "I can't believe it! That is so disgusting! Oh, get me out of here!"

Owen and his mom listened in silence as she

pounded up the stairs. Then Mrs. Foote gave Owen a weak smile.

"I guess this means she doesn't want to be a vet," she said.

His mom sank down into the couch, rested her head against its back, and closed her eyes.

"Having animals isn't for the faint of heart, right, Owen?" she said.

"Right."

For a minute neither of them said anything. Then his mom's eyes popped open and she smiled. "You wanted to tell me about your science project before all of this happened," she said encouragingly. "What did you and Joseph decide?"

"We're going to do something with tadpoles," said Owen. "We got a bunch of them at the swamp this afternoon."

"That's a good idea," said his mom. "What are you going to do with them?"

"I don't know." Owen knew his mom was trying to make him feel better, but it wasn't working. The vet didn't say it was Owen's fault Chuck was sick. But they both knew it was.

Owen hadn't been giving Chuck enough to eat.

"All handfuls aren't the same size" is what the vet said. It seemed to Owen he glanced quickly at Owen's hand when he said it. "I'll give him something to take care of the problem right here and now. But from now on, I'd give him two large handfuls a day."

His mom didn't say, "I told you so." She didn't even act mad when she had to write the vet a check for fifty-five dollars.

Having her be so nice made Owen feel even worse.

"I have an idea, but I haven't talked to Joseph about it yet," he said.

"Why don't you go and call him," said his mom. "We'll have dinner when Dad gets home. And Owen . . ." He stopped in the doorway and turned around. "Don't worry about Chuck. He's fine."

"I know. I'm not."

"Good."

Owen walked slowly up the stairs.

He wasn't worried about Chuck. He was worried about himself. What if he had turned into a lizard wimp? Mr. Wozniak wouldn't want him in his class.

He didn't want kids who just wanted to *look* at the lizards. He wanted kids who were willing to do things with them.

Like feed them. And clean their cages.

And pick them up.

Owen went into his parents' bedroom and sat down on their bed.

Impressing Mr. Wozniak was more important than ever now. Somehow, Owen had to find the nerve to show Joseph the photographs. If Joseph wanted to bolt when he saw them, then Owen had to find a way to make him stay.

If it meant convincing him that frogs with three legs were happier because they could jump higher, that's what Owen was going to do.

He picked up the phone.

6

The Perfect Project

"Wait till you see my volcano," said Ben. He put his lunch tray on the table across from Owen and slid into his seat. "It's awesome."

"There'll probably be about a million volcanoes," said Anthony. "I bet there won't be another blood project."

Owen ignored him. "Maybe you could do something to make it different," he said to Ben. "I always thought it would be cool to build a town at the base of the volcano. The lava could flow over it and destroy it."

"Yeaaah." Ben's eyes lit up. "I could put people in it, too, and show how lava melts them."

"I don't think baking soda and vinegar will produce lava that hot," said Joseph. He put his

crumpled cookie wrapper in his lunch box and pulled out his sandwich. "It'll probably just make them white."

"People will still get the idea," Owen said. "It will be like the volcano that erupted in Italy a long time ago. The one where they found those petrified bodies thousands of years later. The lava covered them so fast, some of the bodies were still at the table, eating."

"That's so amazing," Joseph said.

"Yeah, I bet no one else will have a project like that," said Ben.

"What about blood?" said Anthony. "No one else is going to have blood."

"They'd better, or they'll be dead," Joseph said.

Owen and Ben laughed.

"You know what I mean," said Anthony.

"What's the big deal about blood?" said Owen. "All you're going to have is pictures."

"No, I'm not. My dad's bringing home *real* blood tonight. He dried it and put it on slides. I'm going to have a microscope for people to look through."

"Big deal," Owen said. But he knew dried blood was cool. So was a microscope.

"What are you guys doing?" Ben asked him.

"We got some tadpoles from the swamp," Owen said. "We're doing an experiment about how pollution affects their growth. Right, Joseph?"

"Right."

More than anything, Owen wanted to tell them about the pictures. He knew they'd think a three-legged frog was cool. Anthony might even stop bragging about his dried blood.

But he couldn't. He hadn't showed them to Joseph yet.

Owen had *meant* to show him when they set up their experiment at his house on Saturday. He had the pictures in his drawer, ready to pull out.

It hadn't worked out that way.

When they went up to Owen's room to check on the eggs, they found a bucket full of tadpoles. The water was thick with them.

Joseph had bonded with them right away.

"They look too tiny to even be alive, don't they?" he said, peering into the water. "Some of them even have eyes."

He sounded so excited that Owen knew he couldn't put off telling him about his idea any longer. If Joseph got too fond of the tadpoles, he'd never agree to do anything that might harm them.

"Hey! I have a great idea," Owen said. He hadn't planned on having it come out as if he'd just thought of it. But it did.

"What?" Joseph looked up at him so trustingly, Owen almost stopped. Then he took a deep breath, and went on.

"I just remembered this great article I saw a few months ago," he said. He took his time talking about farmers and crops. He talked about gardeners using fertilizers. He described how they seeped into underground waterways and ponds.

It felt weird. He wasn't exactly lying, but he wasn't telling the truth, either. When he got to the part about the frogs, he was vague.

"What do you mean, they didn't grow normally?" said Joseph.

Owen shrugged. "I guess some of them were kind of funny."

"Funny? You mean deformed?"

Joseph had a weird expression on his face. As if

he knew there was something Owen wasn't saying but he couldn't figure out what it was.

"We won't use *anything* like that much fertilizer," Owen said quickly. "We'll use a tiny amount. Probably nothing will even happen."

"But what if it does?" said Joseph. "I don't want to do anything to hurt these guys. I really think I should do something on my own, Owen."

"No way," Owen said. He felt a sudden sense of panic at the idea of Joseph leaving. "You and I always work together. I'll just use a tiny bit. They'll only be in the water for a week. Nothing will happen, Joseph. I promise."

He said they would use a few of the tadpoles and throw the rest back. He promised they would put the ones in their experiment back as soon as the fair was over.

The minute Joseph agreed, Owen sprang into action. He ran downstairs and got two glass bowls from the kitchen. He went into the garage and put a small amount of fertilizer into a plastic bag.

When he got back upstairs, they put twelve tadpoles in one dish and twelve in another. They wrote CONTROL on a piece of tape and stuck it on one dish.

They wrote FERTILIZER on the other dish.

"Maybe we should write 'doomed' instead," Joseph said.

Usually, Joseph was as enthusiastic about Owen's plans as Owen was. Now he was being very quiet. Owen was eager to get the fertilizer part over. He knew Joseph would relax when they started to write their report.

Owen dipped the tip of a toothpick into the fertilizer and held it up for Joseph to inspect.

"See? There's hardly anything on it."

He quickly swirled it around in the water.

"Do you think they felt anything?" Joseph said anxiously. "I think they're okay, don't you? They look okay."

The tadpoles were flitting around cheerfully. None of them was writhing in pain.

"It's not going to happen that quickly," said Owen. "Probably nothing's going to happen at all. I hope they're at least a little smaller by the science fair, or it won't look like we did *anything*."

"I guess we should write down the first stage," said Joseph.

"Right." Owen grabbed his notebook. He felt much better now that it was over. There was no turning back. "They're in my bedroom, so I'll keep track of them," he said.

"Maybe it should be my job to feed them," said Joseph.

"They're right next to my bed," Owen said. "I'll toss in a bit of food first thing in the morning. You wouldn't believe how easy it is to overfeed these things."

"Then what do I do?" Joseph said.

"You can work on the report and the chart," Owen told him. "You're better at writing than I am."

"Okay." Joseph opened the book they had found on amphibians and took out his box of colored pencils. "How are we going to show the kinds of things that *could* happen?" he asked, hunching over his paper.

Owen stared at the top of Joseph's head. He couldn't show Joseph the pictures right now.

Knowing Joseph, he'd grab the dish and run back to the swamp with it.

Even if Owen convinced him not to, Joseph would feel like a murderer for the entire week. It would ruin their whole project.

Owen needed to stall for time.

Joseph looked up at him. "How are we going to show it?" he asked again.

"We don't have to worry about that right now," Owen said. "We'll look around for something."

"I bet there are lots of pictures," Joseph said.

When Joseph went back to writing, Owen got up and pretended to look for something in his desk. He *still* wasn't lying. He was protecting Joseph. He was protecting their experiment, too.

He'd wait for a few days and see if anything happened. Then he'd show Joseph the pictures.

It sounded like a good plan.

But Joseph beat him to it.

7

A Catastrophe of
Major Proportions

There was a photograph of a frog with one leg. Another of a frog with three legs. One photograph showed a skeleton of a frog with five legs.

In another one, the frog had a leg growing out of its stomach.

The photographs Joseph was putting on the table in front of Owen were even weirder than the ones Owen had found. He was so amazed by how calm Joseph was being about them, all he could do was stare.

"Where did you get them?" he said when Joseph was through.

"They're everywhere." Joseph closed his pack

and put it on the floor. "Once I started looking for information to put in our report, they were easy to find."

"I saw some like these, but I was afraid to show them to you," Owen said. "I thought you'd freak out."

"I kind of did when I first saw them," said Joseph. "Then I realized we *have* to show people these. It's not just a science project—it's important. Your dad needs to stop using fertilizer, Owen."

The minute Joseph said it, Owen knew he was right. With all the thought he'd given to their experiment, he'd never once considered using it to change anything. He'd only thought of it as science.

"And I think you're right," Joseph was saying. "We're not keeping ours in that water long enough to deform them. If I thought we were, I'd probably want to throw them back."

"Yeah," Owen said uneasily. It was weird seeing the pictures lined up this way. What if their tadpoles really did grow two tails? Or two heads? Now that he really thought about it, Owen wasn't sure he'd like that. Especially not in his own bedroom.

"I'm still a little worried they're going to die, though," said Joseph.

"Don't worry, they won't." Owen pushed the pictures into one pile. "We'd better put these on cardboard. I think there's some down in the family room."

At least the problem of the pictures was over, Owen thought with relief as they headed downstairs. All they had to do now was set up their project in the gym on Monday morning.

Then wait till Monday night to see what prize they'd won.

*　　*　　*

"Morning, Owen," Mr. Foote said as he came into the kitchen. He put his hand on the top of Owen's head. "How was your week?"

"Great," said Owen. "How was your trip?"

"Very interesting," said Mr. Foote. He had been at a conference in Arizona for a week. Owen had tried to wait up for him last night, but he fell asleep.

"Where's Mom?" his dad said, pouring a cup of coffee.

"She went to the grocery store," said Owen. "You know her. She likes to get there early on Saturdays, before it gets too crowded."

Mr. Foote took a brown plastic bag off the counter and put it on the table in front of Owen. "I got this for you at a nature museum in Tucson. I didn't have time to wrap it."

"Thanks," Owen said. He pulled out a large green plastic iguana. It had lifelike scales, a long tail, and a pointy head. "This is cool. It looks really real."

"Really real, huh?" Mr. Foote sat down across from him and smiled. "How's your science project going? Monday's the big day, right?"

"We have the two dishes of tadpoles, a few charts, our daily observation notebook, and a report," said Owen. "Joseph wrote most of it. He found some amazing photographs, too."

"What about your fertilizer group? No extra legs or anything?"

"Nope. They're just a little bit smaller than the other ones." Owen held his cereal bowl up to his mouth and drained what was left of the milk. He wiped his mouth with the back of his hand.

"By the way, Dad," he said, "I need to talk to you about your fertilizer."

"I was afraid this was coming."

"I mean it," Owen said. "You've got to stop. You might make the animals in our yard deformed."

"Why'd you have to be a scientist, Owen?" His dad groaned. "Why couldn't you just play video games like other kids?"

"It's not funny," said Owen. "Wait till you see our pictures."

"Could I finish my coffee before you destroy my career as a gardener?"

"Okay. But I'm warning you." Owen put his bowl and spoon in the dishwasher and headed for the stairs.

The three-paneled presentation board was propped up in one corner of his room. THE EFFECTS OF PESTICIDES ON FROG DEVELOPMENT was written in big green letters across the top. Their hypothesis and daily observations were on the left-hand panel. The report and charts were in the middle.

The right-hand panel was covered with their photographs.

Owen had built a small wooden shelf for the dishes. He put it right in the center so everybody would see the tadpoles. They were the one thing that was going to make their project stand out.

Living proof of their whole experiment.

The dish marked FERTILIZER was on the windowsill next to his bed. Owen sprinkled a pinch of frog food over the surface of the water. The fertilized tadpoles nibbled at it frantically.

He headed for the second bowl. It was on the

sill next to his desk. And there were the normal tadpoles . . . dead.

Owen blinked.

There wasn't a sign of life in the dish.

Maybe they're sleeping, Owen thought. He blew on the water. No fluttering tails. No darting movements.

Nothing.

He swished the water around with his finger.

The tadpoles bobbed against one another like driftwood.

"They're *dead!*" Owen shouted. He stared at the lifeless tadpoles in disbelief. How could it be? he thought wildly. What could have happened?

The project was ruined.

"They're dead!" he shouted again. "I can't believe it! All of them! Dead!"

His dad came running up the stairs. Lydia rushed into his room in her nightgown.

"Do you have *any idea* what *time* it is?" she said. "Some of us are trying to sleep."

His dad came into the room and stood next to him. "What happened?"

"The tadpoles are dead," Owen said.

Lydia peered over Owen's shoulder. "You must have put in too much fertilizer," she said.

"These are the normal ones," said Owen. "The fertilized ones are fine."

"Oh. Well, at least some of them are alive."

"The wrong ones, you idiot," said Owen. "That's the whole point. This makes it look like it's healthier to live in poisoned water than in clean water."

"Don't get mad at *me*," Lydia said. "I'm not the murderer."

"Both of you, calm down," said Mr. Foote. He put his hand on Owen's shoulder. "Scientific experiments are supposed to fail sometimes, Owen. When they do, you have to try something else. That's how things get proven. By trial and error."

"We don't have *time* for trial and error," Owen said through clenched teeth. His dad obviously didn't understand. What they were looking at was a catastrophe of major proportions.

Owen started pacing back and forth.

"The fair's the day after tomorrow. . . . The control group's dead. . . . The fertilized group looks normal. . . ."

He stopped and stared at Lydia and Mr. Foote dramatically. "We have no science project," he said. "We're dead."

"You still have the rest of your project," said his dad.

"All it is is a report and some pictures," said Owen. "It'll never win a prize."

"I don't think the fair is about winning," said Mr. Foote. "It's about working on something you're interested in. And learning from it."

"I hate it when you say things like that," said Owen.

"Get real, Dad," Lydia said. "No kid does something just because he's interested in it. Everyone wants to win a prize."

Owen wished they would both go away. He didn't want kind words. He didn't want lame consolation.

What he wanted was to be alone.

The ringing of the doorbell was the final blow.

"It's Joseph." Owen's shoulders slumped as he looked at his dad. "He's coming over so we can put on the finishing touches."

"Maybe you should make little headstones,"

said Lydia. "They're the *ultimate* finishing touch."

"Out." Mr. Foote turned Lydia around by her shoulders and ushered her toward the door. "Owen and Joseph are perfectly capable of handling this on their own," he said.

Owen sank down in front of his project. What was he going to tell Joseph?

The thing Joseph had been dreading all along had happened. He was going to blame Owen and he'd be right. It was Owen's fault. Everything he had touched lately had either gotten sick or died.

First Chuck. Now the tadpoles. Their project was ruined, and it was all his fault.

Owen Foote, mighty scientist.

For the rest of the year he was going to have to listen to Anthony brag about winning another prize. Next year when Anthony talked at Critter Island, Owen was going to have to stand there with all the other losers and listen.

Owen, who loved science more than anything.

The minute Joseph appeared in his doorway, Owen knew it was going to be bad. Joseph looked like he was about to cry, and he hadn't even seen the corpses yet.

Owen took a deep breath. "The control tadpoles are dead," he said.

"I know." Joseph sat down on Owen's bed. "Your dad told me."

"I don't know what happened," said Owen. "They looked fine last night. I must have done something wrong."

"You didn't do anything," Joseph said. "I think it was me."

"What are you talking about?"

"I fed them."

"You did?" Owen stared at him in disbelief.

"I thought about what happened with Chuck," Joseph said. "I didn't want them to starve. So whenever you weren't in the room, I gave them food."

"Just the control tadpoles?"

Joseph nodded. "I didn't want to prolong the misery of the fertilized ones."

"Prolong the misery?" Owen repeated.

"You know what I mean." Joseph's shoulder twitched nervously. "I must have overfed them."

"That's one of the biggest reasons fish and things die," said Owen.

"I know it is. I'm really sorry, Owen."

"*I'm* the one who's sorry," said Owen. His body sagged as the tension of the past few weeks drained out of it.

"I ruined your sneakers," Owen said. "I didn't show you the pictures. . . . I lied about what the fertilizer would do. . . ." The more he confessed, the better he felt. "You never wanted to do this project in the first place, Joseph. I forced you."

"Well, yeah," said Joseph. "But you had to. I'm a wimp about some things."

"Not as much as you used to be, that's for sure," said Owen.

"Thanks."

The air in the room was suddenly clear. It wasn't his fault. Joseph wasn't mad at him. The worst thing that could happen had just happened. Their project might be ruined, but their friendship wasn't.

Because of some dead tadpoles, they were best friends again.

"What are we going to do?" said Joseph.

"I don't know." Owen gazed at their project. "It looks kind of boring without the tadpoles."

They looked at the presentation for a few minutes without talking.

Finally, Joseph said, "I think I know how we can fix it."

"You do?"

"It's kind of weird."

"That's okay. Tell me."

So Joseph talked and Owen listened.

And then they went to work.

8

Outside the Box

"Are you Owen?"

A girl with long brown hair was waiting for him at the gym door. Owen had seen her in the media center with Mr. Wozniak's class.

"Mr. Wozniak wants to see you," she said.

"Go on," his mom said behind him. "Dad and I will wait here for the Trents and catch up to you."

"Tell Joseph to come find me, okay?" Owen said.

The girl had disappeared into the maze of tables and projects lined up inside the gym. Owen spotted the top of her head at the end of a row. He hurried past a mobile of the planets made with colored Ping-Pong balls, a project with beakers and water and dirt, a model airplane with pictures of the Wright brothers, and a volcano.

The volcano had a yellow ribbon on it.

Owen stopped. There was a village made out of clay at its base. The huts and people and animals were covered with white foam. It had to be Ben's.

"Pompeii, Italy. A.D. 76" was written on a label on the front.

Cool, Owen thought. Ben had won third prize.

"Owen! Over here!" a voice called.

It was Mr. Wozniak. He was standing in front of a small table with only one project on it. He was waving.

Owen's stomach did a flip-flop. It was his and Joseph's project, he could tell. He saw the tall green letters. The red arrows pointing to the photographs they had scattered throughout the report.

The purple ribbon at the top.

Purple ribbon? thought Owen as he moved slowly toward it. He had never seen a purple ribbon at the science fair before. Blue was first prize, red was second, and yellow was third.

But *purple?*

Any ribbon was good, right? But what if purple was for "Worst Project of the Fair"?

Or "Better Luck Next Time"?

Owen came to a stop. And where the heck was Joseph?

Before he could turn around to look, Mr. Wozniak came up to him and grabbed his hand.

"Owen Foote, right?" he said. "Great job, Owen."

Mr. Wozniak kept pumping Owen's hand as he said what a fine job Owen and Joseph had done. That he'd never seen a project like it.

"We had to create a 'Special Merit' ribbon, it's such a unique idea," said Mr. Wozniak. "How'd you come up with it?"

A small crowd of kids had clustered around their project. There were a few parents, too. Some of the kids were pointing at the pictures of the frogs and squealing.

Mr. Wozniak finally stopped shaking Owen's hand and stood there, waiting.

"It was really Joseph's idea," said Owen.

Joseph appeared at Owen's side like a miracle. "At the beginning, it was," said Joseph. "Then it was both of ours."

Mr. Wozniak shook Joseph's hand in the same enthusiastic way. Then Owen and Joseph started to explain. Owen told Mr. Wozniak about the

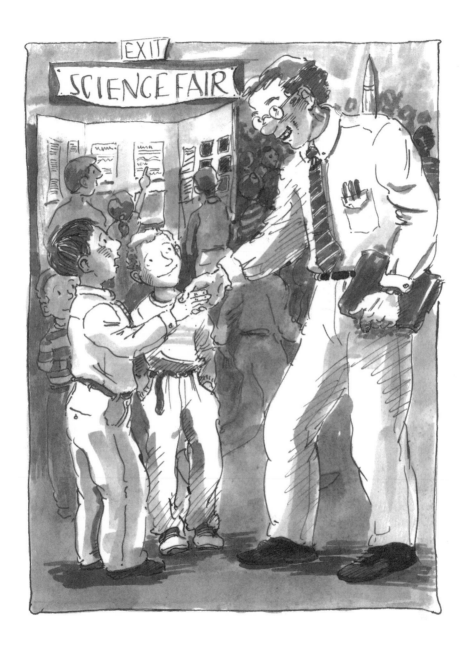

magazine. About remembering his dad's fertilizer. And the swamp.

About the horrible moment he saw the dead tadpoles.

"Then I told him I had fed them," Joseph said.

"And I thought the whole project was ruined," said Owen.

"So I said maybe we should show what had gone wrong."

"Right." Owen gestured toward their presentation board. "So we changed the name to 'The Effects of Interference on a Science Project.'"

"And I posed for some pictures," said Joseph.

He led Owen and Mr. Wozniak closer to the table. In one of the photographs Joseph was tiptoeing in an exaggerated way into Owen's room. In another one he was scattering food over a bowl.

The third photograph was of Mrs. Foote.

It turned out that she had fed the tadpoles, too.

"I'm sorry, Owen," she had confessed guiltily. "I couldn't help myself."

"I know, I know," said Owen. "Joseph said the same thing."

She agreed to pose for the photograph as punishment. In it, she was holding her finger up to her lips like she was asking the audience not to tell on her.

Owen wrote a pledge declaring she would never interfere with a project again and made her sign it. He pasted it to the bottom of the report. There was a red arrow pointing to it.

I, Helen S. Foote, hereby promise never to touch a science project of my son's again. Or else, it said.

"I love the picture of your mom," Mr. Wozniak said with a laugh. "The pledge is a great touch, too."

"Thanks."

"And I hope every person at the fair reads this," said Mr. Wozniak. He pointed to a piece of yellow paper they had added at the last minute.

THE RULES OF WORKING AS A TEAM

- Each member has an equal vote.
- No team member can do anything behind the other member's back.
- Team members should agree to all steps before a project is started.
- Failure to follow these rules could lead to disaster!

"That was Owen's idea," said Joseph.

"Well, it was a good one." Mr. Wozniak put a hand on each of their shoulders. "You boys really thought outside the box," he said. "There are a lot of valuable lessons in this, for kids and parents alike."

Joseph jabbed Owen in the ribs. "Tell him about your uromastyx," he said.

"You have a uromastyx?" said Mr. Wozniak. "I had one of those. He was wild."

"Chuck's a little high strung," said Owen.

"The only way to calm him down is to spend a lot of time with him," Mr. Wozniak said.

"Actually, I haven't been paying that much attention to him since he had a . . . kind of . . . accident in my hand." Owen felt himself blushing.

"That's not a lot of fun, is it?" said Mr. Wozniak. "Makes you nervous about picking them up again."

"And how," Owen said. The relief of knowing that Mr. Wozniak understood the way he felt was enormous.

"Try wearing gloves until Chuck gets used to

you," said Mr. Wozniak. "And bring him in to school sometime. I'd love to see him."

"Sure. Thanks."

The minute Mr. Wozniak left, a group of kids crowded in around Owen and Joseph. They had questions. Lots of questions.

Even without a white lab coat, Owen felt like a real scientist answering them.

9

Side by Side

The liberated tadpoles scattered into the murky water.

"Say hello to your brothers and sisters for me!" Joseph shouted.

"Good luck finding three shoes that match!" yelled Owen.

He shook the last of the water from the plastic dish and scrambled back up the bank to where Joseph was waiting.

"Boy, am I glad that's over," Joseph said.

"Me, too," said Owen.

They started back through the woods.

"I can't believe Anthony's dad called Mr. Wozniak to complain about Anthony only getting second prize," Owen said. "I'd die if my dad did that."

"Your dad wouldn't do it," Joseph said. "Anthony said the soil-erosion project that won stinks."

"That shows you how much Anthony knows," Owen said. "It was cool."

He picked up a sturdy branch to use as a walking stick and began peeling off the bark.

"The gloves my mom got for me are great," Owen said. "It's not as scary now to hold Chuck. He's really calming down."

"I still don't want to hold him," said Joseph.

"It's not just Chuck, is it?" Owen said. He had never realized it before, but he knew it was true. "You don't like any lizards."

"I only like them because you like them," said Joseph. "I don't want to hold them or anything. I'd rather hold my turtle."

"That's the difference between us," Owen said. "No offense, but I think turtles are kind of boring."

"That's why I like them."

Owen was suddenly very happy. The woods had the earthy, damp smell of spring. The tightly wound buds at the end of every branch looked as if they were about to burst. He finished stripping the bark off his stick and jabbed it into the ground ahead of him as he walked.

When they broke out of the underbrush onto the path, Joseph caught up to him so they could walk together.

"You know, I don't care about being in Mr. Wozniak's class as much as you do," Joseph said.

"You don't?"

"Not really. It's the right place for you, but not for me."

"Whose class do you want to be in?"

"Ms. Holt's."

"Really?" Owen was so surprised he stopped walking. Joseph did, too.

"You actually want to sing?" Owen said. "And act in plays?"

"I really do," Joseph said. "I'm going to be in the Chesterfield Voices next year."

"You are?" Owen shook his head in amazement. It was one surprise after another. "But you get nervous when you even talk in front of people."

"I don't when I'm singing or acting," Joseph said. "When I was in that play at camp, I wasn't afraid at all. It was like it wasn't me up there. It was someone else."

"Cool." Owen started to walk again, more slowly this time. Joseph was giving him a lot to think about.

"Maybe you'll be a famous scientist when you grow up, and I'll be a famous actor," said Joseph.

"Yeah." Owen liked that idea. "And when they make a movie about my life, you can play me."

"They'll have to use a double when it's time to hold the lizards," said Joseph.

"Right."

They laughed.

"Want to go to my house and do mazes?" Joseph said.